Librarians

A Level Three Reader

By Charnan Simon

Content Adviser: Andrew Medlar,
Youth Materials Specialist, Chicago Public Library

The
Child's
World®

Published by The Child's World®

P.O. Box 326
Chanhassen, MN 55317-0326
800-599-READ
www.childsworld.com

Photo Credits
© Blaine Harrington/CORBIS: 18
© Cassy Cohan/PhotoEdit: 13
© David Pollack/CORBIS: 21
© Elena Rooraid/PhotoEdit: 26
© Jose Luis Pelaez/CORBIS: 17
© L. C. Diehl/Photo Edit: 14
© LWA-Dann Tardif/CORBIS: 3
© Mark E. Gibson/CORBIS: 25
© Romie Flanagan: 5, 10, 11, 22
© Royalty-Free/CORBIS: 6
© Sean Justice/ImageBank: cover
© Tom Stewart/CORBIS: 29

Editorial Directions, Inc.: E. Russell Primm and Emily J. Dolbear, Editors;
Alice K. Flanagan, Photo Researcher

The Child's World®: Mary Berendes, Publishing Director

Library of Congress Cataloging-in-Publication Data
Simon, Charnan.
  Librarians / by Charnan Simon.
    p. cm. — (Wonder books)
  "A level three reader."
  Summary: An introduction to the work librarians do and some of the
libraries they work in. Includes bibliographical references and index.
  ISBN 1-56766-464-4 (lib. bdg. : alk. paper)
  1. Librarians—Juvenile literature. 2. Libraries—Juvenile literature.
[1. Librarians. 2. Occupations. 3. Libraries.] I. Title. II. Wonder books (Chanhassen, Minn.)
  Z682 .S58 2003
  020'.23—dc21   2002151410

Do you like to read and look
at books? Then you must like
the library!

Libraries are full of wonderful books. Librarians are the people who work in libraries. They help you find just the right book to take home.

A librarian helps a young reader. →

Librarians take care of everything in the library. Hundreds or thousands of books may be in a library. There are many magazines and newspapers, too. You will also find computers, music, and videos in the library.

This library has thousands of books.

Librarians are very busy. They buy books for their libraries. They look in **catalogs** from book **publishers**. They read **reviews** of new books. They talk to people who sell books. Librarians are always reading and learning about new things.

A librarian learns about new books on her computer. →

There are so many magazines to choose from! Librarians pick out newspapers and magazines they think their readers will like. They keep new **issues** on the **shelves**. They store old issues in back rooms.

A boy looks at new magazines at the library.

Librarians give people library cards so they can take books home. The librarian swipes your card and the books into the library computer. Now there is a list of what you have checked out. When you use your library card, you agree to take good care of the books.

A librarian swipes a book into the library computer. →

13

When you return your books, the librarian checks them into the computer. Now everyone knows that you have brought the books back. Then another library worker puts the books back on the shelves—ready for someone else to read.

A boy returns a library book.

Sometimes it is hard to find the right book. Librarians can help! They show you which shelves to look on. They help you use the computer to find what you are looking for.

This librarian teaches a visitor about the library computer. →

17

Sometimes you go to the library to do your homework. Maybe you want to write a report about puppies. The librarian can help you look for information about puppies. He can show you the big **encyclopedias**. He can find magazine articles about puppies.

A librarian works with a student on his report on puppies.

Little children go to the library for story hour. Librarians are good at sharing books and telling stories. Sometimes librarians help children do special crafts. What do you think this story hour is about?

Children enjoy story hour at the library. →

Uh-oh! This book has a torn page. That can happen when books are used a lot. Luckily, librarians know how to mend books so they look almost new.

This librarian knows how to fix library books.

Some librarians work in **community libraries**. They know about books for grown-ups and books for children. Other librarians work in school libraries. These librarians spend most of their time finding books for children.

This librarian works in a school library. →

25

Some librarians don't work in libraries at all. They work in bookmobiles. A bookmobile is a special truck filled with books. It travels to small towns and villages that don't have their own libraries. People check out books from bookmobiles just as they do from regular libraries.

Librarians study hard at special library schools. They learn all they can about how to bring books and people together. Librarians and books—they are both pretty wonderful!

Librarians work hard! →

Glossary

catalogs (KAT-uh-logz)
Catalogs list things you can buy from a company.

community libraries
(kuh-MYOO-nuh-tee LYE-brer-eez)
Community libraries are libraries used by all the people living in the same place or neighborhood.

encyclopedias (en-sye-kloh-PEE-dee-uhs)
Encyclopedias are books or sets of books that give information about many different subjects.

issues (ISH-ooz)
Issues are copies of a magazine or newspaper sent out at one time. Many magazines have a new issue every month.

publishers (PUHB-lish-urs)
Publishers are the people and companies who make and sell books.

reviews (ri-VYOOZ)
Reviews are reports of a book written by someone who has read it carefully.

shelves (SHELVZ)
Shelves are flat, stacked boards used for storing things such as books.

Index

To Find Out More

Books

Burby, Liza N. *A Day in the Life of a Librarian.* New York: PowerKids Press, 1999.

Flanagan, Alice K. *Ms. Davison, Our Librarian.* Danbury, Conn.: Children's Press, 1997.

Gorman, Jacqueline Laks. *Librarian.* Milwaukee, Wis.: Gareth Stevens, 2002.

Kottke, Jan. *A Day with a Librarian.* Danbury, Conn.: Scholastic Library Publishing, 2000.

Web Sites

Visit our homepage for lots of links about librarians:
http://www.childsworld.com/links.html

Note to Parents, Teachers, and Librarians:
We routinely verify our Web links to make sure they're safe, active sites—so encourage your readers to check them out!

Note to Parents and Educators

Welcome to Wonder Books®! These books provide text at three different levels for beginning readers to practice and strengthen their reading skills. Additionally, the use of nonfiction text provides readers the valuable opportunity to *read to learn*, not just to learn to read.

These leveled readers allow children to choose books at their level of reading confidence and performance. Nonfiction Level One books offer beginning readers simple language, word choice, and sentence structure as well as a word list. Nonfiction Level Two books feature slightly more difficult vocabulary, longer sentences, and longer total text. In the back of each Nonfiction Level Two book are an index and a list of books and Web sites for finding out more information. Nonfiction Level Three books continue to extend word choice and length of text. In the back of each Nonfiction Level Three book are a glossary, an index, and a list of books and Web sites for further research.

State and national standards in reading and language arts emphasize using nonfiction at all levels of reading development. Wonder Books® fill the historical void in nonfiction material for primary grade readers with the additional benefit of a leveled text.

About the Author

Charnan Simon lives in Madison, Wisconsin, with her husband and two daughters. She began her publishing career in the children's book division of Little, Brown and Company, and then became an editor of *Cricket Magazine*. Simon is currently a contributing editor for *Click Magazine* and an author with more than 40 books to her credit. When she is not busy writing, she enjoys reading, gardening, and spending time with her family.